DATE DUE

**Three (3) week loans are subject
to recall after one week**

NOV − 5 1992	SEP 2 6 1994	APR 2 8 1995
DEC 1 0 1992	OCT 1 7 1994	
DEC 2 1 1992	OCT 2 8 1994	
DEC 2 9 1992	NOV 8 1994	
FEB 1 6 1993	DEC 2 3 1994	
MAR 1 8 1993	JAN 2 1 1995	
MAR 2 4 1993	FEB 1 3 1995	
APR − 5 1994	MAR 1 9 1995	
MAY 2 1994	MAR 3 1 1995	

APR − 6 1992

I HAVE TO SEE THIS!

Story
by Richard
Thompson

Art
by Eugenie
Fernandes

Annick Press, Toronto Canada

Annick Press gratefully acknowledges
the support of the Canada Council and
The Ontario Arts Council

Canadian Cataloguing in Publication Data

Thompson, Richard, 1951–
  I have to see this

(The Jesse adventures)
ISBN 1-55037-015-4 (bound) ISBN 1 55037 014 6
(pbk.)

I. Fernandes, Eugenie, 1943–   . II. Title.
III. Series: Thompson, Richard, 1951–   . The Jesse
adventures.

PS8589.H65I15 1988   jC813'.54   C88-93492-1
PZ7.T46I 1988

  Distributed in Canada and the USA by:
  Firefly Books Ltd.,
  3520 Pharmacy Ave., *Unit 1c*
  Scarborough, Ontario
  M1W 2T8

  Printed and bound in Canada
  by D.W. Friesen & Sons

For Margaret

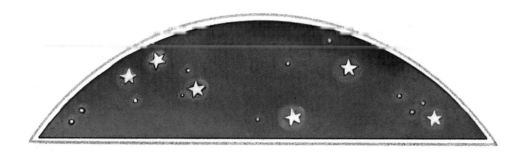

On a starry evening in the middle of winter, Jesse and her dad went for a walk. Well, Jesse's dad went for a walk; Jesse went for a ride on his shoulders.

"I am high up!" she exclaimed.

"What can you see from up there?" asked her dad.

Jesse looked around. "I can see stars and the moon!" she said. "And there's the Man in the Moon."

"Oh?" said her dad in surprise. "What's he doing?"

"He is feeding the pigs," said Jesse.

"Oh?" said her dad.

"He has blue eyes," said Jesse. "And brown hair. He is wearing a suit."

"What kind of suit?" asked her dad.

"Pink and orange and purple and green," said Jesse.

"I have to see this," said her dad.

"You aren't high up," said Jesse.

"But I want to see!" insisted her dad. "Can I sit on your shoulders?"

"No," said Jesse, "you are too big!"

"I have an idea," said her dad. He lifted her down. He climbed up on a mail box. He looked all around. He could see some stars, and he could see the moon, but no Man in the Moon.

"Maybe they went in the house," said Jesse. "Let me look."

Her dad lifted her back onto his shoulders.

"I can see them," said Jesse. "The Mommy in the Moon and the Baby in the Moon are there, too."

"I didn't see anything," said her dad. "What are they doing?"

"The pigs are teaching the Mommy in the Moon and the Baby in the Moon how to oink."

"I have to see this," said her dad. "I have an idea."

He lifted Jesse down. He climbed up a tree.
"I can't see them," he puffed.
"Maybe it is too cloudy now," said Jesse.
"Let me look."
Jesse's dad lifted her onto his shoulders.
"I can see them," she said.
"What are they doing?"
asked her dad.
"The Man in the Moon and
the Mommy in the Moon
are dancing," said Jesse.

"The Baby in the Moon and the pigs are oinking the song."

"What are they oinking?" asked her dad.

"It sounds like 'Sur le Pont d'Avignon'."
"I have to see this!" said her dad.

He lifted her down and started climbing up a lamp post.

While he was climbing, a policeman came up to Jesse.

"Are you lost, little girl?" he asked.

"No," said Jesse, "I'm with my daddy."

"Where is he?" asked the policeman.

"Up there," said Jesse, pointing. "He's watching the Man in the Moon and the Mommy in the Moon dancing."

The policeman looked up. "I think you'd better come down from there, mister," he called.

On the way home, Jesse asked
"Did you see them dancing, Dad?"
He didn't feel like saying anything.
"They aren't dancing anymore,"
said Jesse. "The pigs are in their
sleeping bags."

"The Mommy in the Moon is making popcorn.

And the Man in the Moon and the
Baby in the Moon are going for a walk."
"Hm," said her dad.

"Are you sad about not seeing the Man in the Moon?"

"Just a little," said her dad.

"Maybe you can see them next time," said Jesse.

"I don't think so," said her dad. "No one has shoulders that I can sit on."

"Sometimes I dream about the Man in the Moon and the Mommy in the Moon and the Baby in the Moon and the singing pigs," said Jesse. "Maybe you will see them when you dream tonight."